SCORPIONS

YUMIKO KURAHASHI

SCORPIONS

TRANSLATED BY MICHAEL DAY

WAKEFIELD PRESS / CAMBRIDGE, MASSACHUSETTS

Wakefield Press, P.O. Box 425645, Cambridge, MA 02142

First published in Japan in 1968 by Tokuma Shoten Publishing Co., Ltd., Tokyo. English translation rights arranged with Sayaka Nakajima through Japan Foreign-Rights Centre.

This book was set in Garamond Premier Pro and Helvetica Neue Pro by Wakefield Press. Printed and bound by Versa Press in the United States of America.

ISBN: 978-1-962728-10-2

Available through D.A.P./Distributed Art Publishers
75 Broad Street, Suite 630
New York, New York 10004
Tel: (212) 627-1999
Fax: (212) 627-9484

10 9 8 7 6 5 4 3 2

TRANSLATOR'S INTRODUCTION

> My literature is like a "cancer" that parasitically attacks, devours, and destroys the orthodox, old type of literature.
>
> Yumiko Kurahashi

Yumiko Kurahashi (1935–2005) is a Japanese author whose works of experimental, genre-bending fiction consistently question or negate literary and social norms. Her fantasy-infused "anti-novels" are filled with graphic violence and every sort of outlandish sexual act from incest to bestiality to necrophilia to sex with aliens and ghosts. An intellectual outlaw who spent her career on the fringes of the Japanese literary establishment, she was accused of everything from immorality to superficiality to plagiarism, remaining a dedicated parodist, pastiche artist, prankster, and provocateur. Her work is rooted in a fierce vision of female sexuality as a devouring, destructive force, making it a threat to heteronormativity, homogeneity, and squareness of all stripes.

This novella, first published in a journal in 1963 when Kurahashi was just twenty-seven, shows her at her most radical and colorful. In a wild, experimental prose style, using the framing device of a psychological report, she tells the tale of K and L, incestuous twins who play a role in a series of horrifying crimes culminating in the murder of their mother. The novella is an early encapsulation of a personal mythology Kurahashi developed as a pastiche of Plato that would come to define her work. The experimentation with form and style and confrontational subject matter register as provocative even sixty years on. Few have taken up the gauntlet thrown down in these pages.

•

Kurahashi's rebellion may have begun when she refused to join her father's dental practice. He wanted her to stay on in Kōchi, Shikoku as his assistant, and though she obtained a hygienist's certificate—an experience that inspired the story "Kai no naka" ("Inside the Shell"), about an attempted proletarian revolution at a girls' dental school dormitory—what she actually did next was study literature without her parents' knowledge or consent. She was admitted to the French department at Meiji University, where she wrote her graduation thesis on Jean-Paul Sartre's *Being and Nothingness*. Her short story "Parutai" ("Partei"), a satire of radical student politics in which a scornful female narrator withdraws from an unnamed party, was nominated for, but did not win, the prestigious Akutagawa Prize in 1960 while she was still a student. Ken Hirano, a well-known critic, prominently championed her, as he had Kenzaburō Ōe. The following year, her story "Natsu no owari" (The end of summer), in which two sisters plot to kill a shared male lover, was nominated for the prize. Again, it failed to win, but all this drew attention and controversy to Kurahashi, with debates on the literary merit and subject matter of her work playing out in journals for months. It is clear that at least some of the criticism was driven by Kurahashi's gender—not everyone was comfortable with works of biting political satire, or works filled with violence and wild sex, written by a young woman.[1]

In 1961 she published her first novel, *Kurai tabi* (A dark journey), which is written in the second person and strongly echoes Michel Butor's 1957 *La modification* (*A Change of Heart*); a debate on pastiche and plagiarism exploded in the press, with Kurahashi responding that of course she was inspired by Butor, defending mimicry as valid, and questioning the existence of originality.[2] Other important works of hers from the 1960s include *Scorpions* (1963) and *Seishōjo* (Holy daughter, 1965), a Jean Genet–inspired portrait of a criminal young woman in an incestuous relationship with her father.

From 1966 to 1967, she studied at the University of Iowa on a Fulbright scholarship. Her characteristically contrarian next move was to release the uncharacteristically realist novella *Vaajinia* (Virginia, 1968) based on her experiences in Iowa. In 1970, she published *Yume no ukihashi* (Floating bridge of dreams), the first installment in what would become a lengthy series of fantastical stories and novels featuring a narrator named Keiko. She was fairly inactive throughout the 1970s but resumed literary production with the second installment in the series, *Shiro no naka no shiro* (A castle within a castle), in 1979. Kurahashi is especially recognized for her 1984 short story collection *Otona no tame no zankoku dōwa* (Cruel fairy tales for adults), which consists of grotesque, erotic retellings of myths and fairy tales from around the world, and *Amanonkoku okanki* (Record of a journey to the Amanons, 1987), an avant-garde science-fiction epic in which a lone male missionary is confronted with the horror of a land inhabited solely by women. Kurahashi also translated children's literature, including many works by Shel Silverstein and Antoine de Saint-Exupéry's *The Little Prince*, the latter the final work she completed in her lifetime.

Since Kurahashi's death in 2005, many of her works, including the early novels *Kurai tabi* and *Seishōjo*, have been reprinted. Successful contemporary authors such as Hiromi Kawakami (*Strange Weather in Tokyo*) and Yōko Ogawa (*The Memory Police*) have named her as an influence.[3] In 2007, Kazuki Sakuraba won the Naoki Prize, one of Japan's most prestigious literary awards, for *Watashi no otoko* (My man), a novel about father-daughter incest that shows the clear influence of Kurahashi's *Seishōjo*, which Sakuraba calls "a dangerous, wild, fearless, crazy, stunningly great girls' novel that will eternally endure."[4] In Japan, Kurahashi remains a cult figure, a writer's writer who continues to have a significant influence over a small but devoted group of followers.

Kurahashi's work can be seen as part of an "anti-realist," anti-modern trend in Japanese fiction, along with authors such as Sōseki Natsume, Kōbō Abe, Kyōka Izumi, and Haruki Murakami.[5] But as Kurahashi puts it, "When speaking about what kind of novels I write, it is necessary above all else to discuss what my novels 'are not.'"[6] This reflects the fact that her writing consistently tries not to illuminate truth, but to obscure it by drawing readers into fantastical labyrinths; not to define human nature, but to show that it cannot be known; not to make concrete statements, but to corrode the foundation on which concrete statements rest—the cold, chauvinist logic of the "real" world. Drawing inspiration from the French *anti-roman*, she sets forth a consciously constructed ideal she calls the "anti-novel," seeking to depict an "anti-world" in which unknowable characters do nothing, mimicry triumphs over originality, fantasy is more real than fact, and the sexual norms and values of the real world are gutted.

•

In a 1966 essay entitled "Shōsetsu no meiro to hiteisei" (Negativity and the labyrinth of literature), she writes, "At an uncertain time, in a place that is nowhere, somebody who is no one, for no reason, is about to do something—and in the end does nothing: This is my ideal of the novel."[7]

In Kurahashi's anti-novels, plots are often lifted from myth or other works of literature, if they exist in the traditional sense. Women, children, criminals, and other people who hold subservient positions in the real world are elevated to elite positions. In her early fiction at least, characters are typically referred to by initials such as K, L, and M, dehumanizing them, an approach that shows the influence of Kafka. Far from serving as vehicles for illuminating human nature, her characters become less and less knowable as the non-events of the story fail to unfold.

•

Although Kurahashi hated being called a "woman writer," if the anti-world had a shape, it would be something that sinks in rather than something that sticks out, like the Japanese kanji *boko/ō* (凹 [instead of *deko/totsu* (凸)]). Like a vagina. Atsuko Sakaki writes, "Kurahashi's fiction does not impose any manifesto onto the 'real' world; it rather suggests the nothingness which it contains, just as women have a womb inside them, instead of a penis sticking out."[8] Her writing destroys by drawing in and devouring, not by striking with worldly tools such as logical argumentation. Indirect weapons such as illusion, mimicry, distraction, fantasy, and parody do great damage in her skilled hands.

In *Scorpions*, although the twins commit their crimes together, the female half of the duo, L, is the driving force in more than one way. While mostly not taking an actively violent role, she consciously manipulates sexuality to drive two men to murder one another, and she decides how her mother will die.

Kurahashi's vision of vicious femininity is clearly pitted squarely against patriarchy, but it is not appropriate to call her a feminist. Faye Yuan Kleeman points out that Kurahashi's views on gender politics are "volatile and elusive," and her consistent negative depictions of mothers—this novella includes a very memorable one—can even seem misogynistic.[9] In her views on gender, as in so many other areas, Kurahashi is an iconoclast above all else.

•

The concepts of the anti-novel and the anti-world which are key to Kurahashi's artistic vision originate from titans of radical twentieth-century French literature Jean-Paul Sartre and Jean Genet. Kurahashi, who deeply admired French literature and believed all art was imitation, freely adapted these concepts for her own purposes. Sartre introduced the term *anti-roman* to the modern literary world in 1948.[10] In her essay "On the Anti-Novel," Kurahashi writes, "We should recognize that there may be such a monstrous thing as a novel which resembles a false poem written in false prose; it could be said that Jean Genet wrote such novels."[11] This terminology too is drawn from Sartre, who states, "Genet's works are false novels written in false prose."[12] Genet makes the affinity between his Parisian criminal underworld and Kurahashi's anti-world impossible to ignore when he writes, "Repudiating the virtues of your world, criminals agree hopelessly to organize a forbidden universe," that is, an anti-world whose members stand in opposition to the values of society.[13] Kurahashi has expressed admiration for both Sartre and Genet and called copying a "royal road."[14]

Kurahashi's fascination with incest, an aspect of her work that maintains undiminished power to shock, is also linked to her admiration for Genet and Sartre. In a 1966 essay entitled "Insesuto ni tsuite" (On incest), she writes, "Incest as it actually occurs in society is almost without exception nothing but a vile, filthy act (or so goes my stubborn prejudice) and the reason I write about incest is because I feel drawn to the topic of how to sanctify it."[15] Here she is in dialogue with Sartre's *Saint Genet*, which holds up Genet's criminal behavior as holy. Kurahashi's intent may be partly to provoke, but it is definitely not to promote incest; instead, she is drawn to the imaginative challenge of "sanctifying" it in the context of a subversive, fantastical anti-world, accepting the imaginative challenge proposed by Genet and taking it further.

In this way, her work can be seen as a conscious pastiche, even a kind of warped copy, of the most radical French literature of her time. Kurahashi would have received this as praise.

•

This work is a copy in many ways.

A gifted parodist, Kurahashi's subversive powers extend to myth and archetype, the building blocks of stories. *Scorpions* is a retelling of the Greek myth of Electra and Orestes, in which the two siblings murder their mother Clytemnestra. Kurahashi was enchanted with this myth and adapted it on multiple occasions, including in *Scorpions*, "Himawari no ie" (The house of sunflowers), and *Seishōjo*.

This work is also shaped by a private mythology Kurahashi developed as a subversive spin on Plato. She describes this personal myth as follows:

> Plato proposes that man and woman once embraced each other, forming a single body, but according to my own mythology, K and L once embraced each other within the same womb. . . . After birth, they separated into two bodies, but their consciousnesses are composed of the same elements and they possess the same memory of the time they spent embracing in amniotic fluid. Though this memory is ordinarily absorbed into their bodies, they can excrete it like an invisible gas at any time and become one again. In other words, the consciousnesses of K and L are able to embrace in a nonphysical sense. This is my mythic love, my Platonic love. This is supremely vulgar love, and of course, it is impossible. . . . The defining attributes of these twin gods which appear in my novels can be summed up by stating that they are beings which aim for nonexistence, or rather that they are passive yet aware.[16]

This concept is represented literally in a scene in *Scorpions* in which the twins swim in the filthy water of a decrepit harbor. As an enactment of Kurahashi's reconfiguration of Platonic myth, this scene is a copy of a copy:

> Submerged to our necks, we leisurely swam. K's face was so pale . . . I was suddenly struck by the terrifying sense that we were drifting in murky amniotic fluid. Yes, perhaps a submerged

memory of K and me embracing in the OLD BAG's womb had resurfaced here, twenty years later, from the chill water of this uncanny harbor.

K and L also appear, occasionally unnamed, in stories and novels such as "Seikazoku" ("The Holy Family"), *Seishōjo*, "Ai no inga" ("A Negative Portrait of Love"), "Himawari no ie," and "Uchūjin" ("An Extraterrestrial"), to name just a few, making *Scorpions* an early encapsulation of a theme key to Kurahashi's work. They typically are in an incestuous relationship with each other and sometimes with their parents. The twins are copies of each other and their stories are copies of other stories.

Luciana Cardi points out that "Kurahashi retells Greek mythological motifs to produce new narrative forms where the 'original discourse' and its 'imitation' coexist, as the narration continuously shifts between the ancient myth and its modern retelling."[17] Paradoxically, since myth has always been transmitted through continuous retelling, a process in which "originality" itself is in question, this marks Kurahashi as a truly authentic myth-maker.

There is yet one more way in which this work is a pastiche. Kurahashi reveals that she patterned it after Osamu Dazai's classic novel *The Setting Sun* (1947), which depicts an aristocratic family in decline after World War II.[18] The parallels in this case are for the most part not obvious, but Dazai's work does deeply shape this one: commonalities include the declining status of K and L's family, as revealed by subtle mentions of depleted fortunes ("Our family had once borne the barbaric title of bourgeois"), the premise of a daughter and son living with their invalid mother, and the class complications surrounding the modern-minded daughter's marriage aspirations or lack thereof. In one obvious similarity, the works share scenes of the mother consuming soup in a, shall we say, idiosyncratic way. Dazai's work does not contain any colorfully monstrous murders, which are pure products of Kurahashi's outrageous imagination.

•

The specter of a radical political party hovers over many of Kurahashi's novels and stories. Sometimes named and sometimes not, the "party" is always a target of scorn and ridicule. Examples include her best-known story "Partei," a satirical tale of political nonaction; "Inside the Shell," concerning an aborted revolution at a girls' dental school; *Sumiyakisuto Q no bōken* (*The Adventures of Sumiyakist Q*), which ridicules communism in the guise of the absurd fictional ideology of "sumiyakism"; and many other works. Though more subtly, the presence of politics is also felt in *Scorpions.*

The novella makes several references to the twins' former membership in the All-Japan Student Association. This real-life far-left organization played a role in such activities as the violent 1959–1960 protests against the US–Japan Security Treaty. Kurahashi was a student during this time of campus political agitation and apparently was nonplussed by it; that she had the type of personality that resisted joining groups seems clear. She sums up her views on politics as follows:

> If it is the case that there are many ideological flags in the world—here Marxism, there Maoism—and that people are required to swarm beneath one of them in order to continue living, then a person cannot help but embrace one or more ideologies. . . . People should be able to walk freely among this assemblage of flags without believing in ideologies.[19]

Scorn for mass action is baked into her artistic vision. If the twins in *Scorpions* represented any particular political position, this would not fulfill the condition that the protagonist of the anti-novel "in the end does nothing," but they remain unattached to any ideology, and the premise is fulfilled. They take pleasure in watching protestors burn the car they inherited from their bourgeois father, showing a preference for pure destruction over politics. Says L, "Don't doubt we burned with the urge to kill from the moment we were born. In fact, it was this alone that sustained us." According to the inverted logic of the anti-world, these aloof, hostile twins are sanctified as elites.

•

A bit about the novella's style and voice. Like most of Kurahashi's early fiction, *Scorpions* is written in a colorful, confrontational prose style.

In *Scorpions*, numerous words and phrases are marked with *bōten* (﹅), comma-like emphasis marks that appear to the right of the text. Although a conventional typographical method, this tactic is used extensively in Kurahashi's early work to create a jarring visual effect in which certain words and phrases leap off the page. In this translation, such words and phrases are represented in caps—"RED PIG," "MADAME," etc.—to approximate this effect.

The text also contains a smattering of English and French phrases, written in either katakana script (something like Japanese italics) or Roman script, when Japanese equivalents would have done the job. I have generally used italicized French terms in these cases—*embrasse*, *douzaine*, etc. In one example, "give and take," I have translated an English term into French as *donner et prendre* to re-foreignize it for English-language readers. Japanese readers in 1963 must have been surprised to find such terms, along with "fellatio" and "cunnilingus," appearing in Roman script in the pages of a Japanese journal.

The biblical passages, in Japanese translation in the original, present a translator with endless options, among which I settled on the original King James Version with uncorrected antique spellings as a fittingly defamiliarizing form of a text everyone knows.

Another interesting aspect of the voice of the novella: it is written mainly in the *-desu -masu* form, which is both formal, as appropriate to a patient addressing a doctor, and traditionally preferred by women. It is also sprinkled with informal, clearly female speech (using the sentence-ending particle *wa*), giving some of the most horrific descriptions in the text a glib, girlish tone. Of course, in English, there is no way to mark the voice as specifically female, so I have settled on a subtle yet jarring mix of registers as the best available equivalent.

•

Kurahashi, who once wrote an essay entitled "Literature as Poison," wanted the poisonous strains of thought she wove into her work to worm their way into the real world and undermine its logic. Right now, that process is about to start through your contact with this novella. Like a fatal swim in a churning sea—one of the means by which the twins murder—may this most unusual novella leave you indelibly marred by the impression of an anti-world which, as a concave thing that sinks into itself, destroys without leaving a mark.

NOTES

1. Among the *positive* reactions is this gem by a male critic: "When I read the works of Kurahashi, I am filled with admiration for her intellect. The ranks of women writers . . . who, for the most part rely on emotion, are not devoid of intellect. However, I cannot help but think there is something different about Kurahashi's intelligence or, more colloquially, her smarts, which sets her apart from other women. . . . Kurahashi's brain is more masculine, or androgynous. You could even say that it has uniquely evolved, even more than the average man's." See Joan E. Ericson, *Be a Woman: Hayashi Fumiko and Modern Japanese Women's Literature* (Honolulu: University of Hawai'i Press, 1997), 32.

2. For details on the debate, see Atsuko Sakaki, "The Intertextual Novel and the Interrelational Self: Kurahashi Yumiko, A Japanese Postmodernist" (PhD diss., The University of British Columbia, 1992), 36–46.

3. Hiromi Kawakami 川上弘美 and Kazuki Sakuraba 桜庭一樹, "Taidan: Kawakami Hiromi x Sakuraba Kazuki" 対談: 川上弘美×桜庭一樹 [In conversation: Hiromi Kawakami and Kazuki Sakuraba], in *Kurahashi Yumiko: Mugen no dokusō* 倉橋由美子: 夢幻の毒想 [Yumiko Kurahashi: Poisonous visions] (Kawade shobō shinsha, 2008); Yōko Ogawa 小川洋子 and Yōko Hiramatsu 平松洋子, "*Kurai tabi* ga oshiete kureta, itami o tomonau jiishiki no tabi" 暗い旅が教えてくれた、痛みを伴う自意識の旅 [The painful journey to self-awareness as taught by *A Dark Journey*], in *Yōko-san no hondana* 洋子さんの本棚 [The Yokos' bookshelf] (Shūeisha, 2017).

4. Kazuki Sakuraba 桜庭一樹, "Kaisetsu" 解説 [Afterword], in *Seishōjo* 聖少女 [Holy daughter] (Shinchō bunko, 2008).

5. Susan J. Napier, *The Fantastic in Modern Japanese Literature: The Subversion of Modernity* (London: Routledge, 1996).

6. Yumiko Kurahashi 倉橋由美子, "Shōsetsu no meiro to hiteisei" 小説の迷路と否定性 [Negativity and the labyrinth of literature], in *Watashi no naka no kare e* わたしのなかのかれへ [To he who dwells within me] (Kōdansha, 1970), 285–296.

7. Kurahashi, "Shōsetsu no meiro to hiteisei," quoted in Dennis Keene, introduction to "To Die at the Estuary" by Yumiko Kurahashi, in *Contemporary Japanese Literature: An Anthology of Fiction, Film, and Other Writing Since 1945*, ed. Howard Hibbett (Knopf, 1977), 247–281. All other translations in this introduction are mine.

8. Sakaki, "The Intertextual Novel and the Interrelational Self," 11.

9. Faye Yuan Kleeman, "Sexual Politics and Sexual Poetics in Kurahashi Yumiko's *Cruel Fairy Tales for Adults*," in *Constructions and Confrontations: Changing Representations of Women and Feminisms, East and West: Selected Essays*, eds. Cristina Bacchilega and Cornelia N. Moore (Honolulu: University of Hawai'i Press, 1997), 150–158.

10. Jean-Paul Sartre, preface to *Portrait of a Man Unknown*, by Nathalie Sarraute, trans. Maria Jolas (New York: George Braziller, 1958), vii–xiv.

11. Yumiko Kurahashi 倉橋由美子, "Han-shōsetsu ron" 反小説論 [On the anti-novel], in *Meiro no tabibito* 迷路の旅人 [A traveler in the labyrinth] (Kōdansha, 1972), 9–120.

12. Jean-Paul Sartre, *Saint Genet*, trans. Bernard Frechtman (New York: George Braziller, 1963), 425.

13. Jean Genet, *The Thief's Journal*, trans. Bernard Frechtman (Paris: Olympia Press, 2008), 5.

14. Yumiko Kurahashi 倉橋由美子, "Sakusha kara anata e" 作者からあなたへ [From the author to you], in *Kurai tabi* 暗い旅 [A dark journey] (Shinchō bunko, 1971), 238–239.

15. Yumiko Kurahashi 倉橋由美子, "Insesuto ni tsuite" インセストについて [On incest], in *Watashi no naka no kare e*, 254–256.

16. Yumiko Kurahashi 倉橋由美子, "Sakuhin nōto" 作品ノート [Story notes], "Doko ni mo nai basho" どこにもない場所 [A place that is nowhere], in *Kurahashi Yumiko zensakuhin* 倉橋由美子全作品 [The complete works of Yumiko Kurahashi] (Shinchōsha, 1975), 4: 253–260.

17. Luciana Cardi, "Challenging the Traditional Notion of Japanese Novel: Greek Myth in Kurahashi Yumiko's *Amanonkoku ōkanki*," *Cogito* 4, no. 1 (2012).

18. Yumiko Kurahashi 倉橋由美子, "Sakuhin nōto" 作品ノート [Story notes], *Sasori-tachi* 蠍たち [Scorpions], in *Kurahashi Yumiko zensakuhin*, 4: 253–260.

19. Kurahashi, "Han-shōsetsu ron."

SCORPIONS

(i) This report, which was commissioned by T District Court, consists of a transcript of an interview with L, a defendant on trial for the murder of her mother. Prior to the interview, a brief visual examination and vaginal inspection were performed; the individual concerned, a twenty-year-old woman, is developing normally and free from gynecological symptoms.

(ii) Interviewee profile

L.M., twenty years of age, unmarried. Daughter of M, former CEO of C Mining Corporation (deceased). Former member of the Central Executive Committee of the All-Japan Student Association, an organ of the Japanese Communist Party. Currently enrolled in the French Literature Department, T University Faculty of Letters.

(iii) Our initial plan was to conduct a Ravonal Interview, but the interviewee objected vehemently and insisted on making a verbal statement. Throughout the statement, which was delivered from 1:00 p.m. to 4:00 p.m. on 10 October, the interviewee maintained a tone that might be described as articulate and upbeat. The statement was recorded on tape and transcribed from the recording by Y.T., research assistant at T University Faculty of Medicine.

(iv) Note that K (L's brother/fraternal twin), who likewise faces murder charges, refused to be interviewed and is presently composing a written statement. The record of the interview with L and K's written statement will be used to complete a psychological evaluation of the two individuals concerned.

F.K., Assistant Professor, T University Faculty of Medicine

Tell us all about what happened over the summer, you say. Okay, for the sake of your psychological evaluation for the court, I will. Since you're planning on labeling me schizophrenic and getting me released to a hospital—isn't that right? Or is your aim to identify within me a uniquely modern anguish, pluck it out with tweezers, and display it to the world with an accusatory smirk? You are the perfect image of a humanist, you know, with your slicked-back hair and those glasses. And you're young, only a few years older than us, perhaps *une douzaine*. What is K doing now? Is he writing? Reading K's stories would be so much more interesting than making those scribbles on my medical chart . . . but since you insist, I'll begin. First, let me tell you about the RED PIG—that is, S. One dusty afternoon in July, the phone rang. It was the RED PIG. He explained that he wished to visit, so I alerted K, and we confined the MADAME to the HOUSE OF WORSHIP in the yard. Three years or so earlier, the MADAME had renovated a storage shed, turning it into a kind of shrine where she worshipped a god of her own invention. By the MADAME, I mean our mother—so we had referred to her since she had become pious and roly-poly. She herself was pleased by this nickname, and given the turn things had taken, we could not bring ourselves to call her mother. To K and me, she was simply the OLD BAG. The OLD BAG had indeed grown fat, as if from gorging on malevolent spirits.

The RED PIG arrived shortly in a white sportscar with a pointed nose. "Is your mother out?" he asked, and I answered, "Sadly, she is." S too was amply proportioned, and helping him remove his topcoat was like flaying a portly animal. Just then, K appeared, wearing an expression so exaggeratedly solemn that I struggled not to laugh: "We had to lock her up. Recently, she hasn't been in her right mind. She's a menace to the community." At this, the RED PIG chuckled. "Hahaha, well, this heat could drive anyone nuts." It was indeed a hot day, and we were in the reception room, which was warmed by the afternoon sun. It was so hot sweat welled up from the soles of your feet, your eyes, and even seemingly the windowsills, and S's tongue lolled out like that of a tired service dog. He wanted to hire me as secretary, he explained, panting. He had gone to university with our father, who had taken him under his wing, protected him, and now, S explained, he wanted to return the favor. S was president of a large publishing company. Nonetheless, he was a nobody compared to our father, who had been a towering figure in the world of business. Our family had once borne the barbaric title of bourgeois. S was a stout, sturdily built, wealthy man from a decrepit country town, a man who knew nothing of the spiritual aristocracy to which we belonged. He stood somewhat shorter than me, and while dabbing with a handkerchief at a face reddened from too much golf and liquor, he launched into stories of the OLD BAG in her youth, referring to her as Mariko. K and I kicked each other desperately beneath the table, only barely restraining laughter. This corpulent gentleman spun his tale with tender affection, revealing that he had once been enamored of this girl Mariko. Just then, a sort of groan issued from the HOUSE OF WORSHIP in the backyard—it was Mariko herself. The RED PIG asked, Are you keeping an animal or something back there? K and I answered in unison, "Yes, a pig, or something." You may begin work tomorrow, said the RED PIG, leaving the melon he had brought as a present on his way out. We made short work of the melon, then peeked inside the storage shed that the OLD BAG had converted for religious use. On the verge of fainting from ecstasy, the OLD BAG clawed at the crucifixion image on the wall. I wiped away the piss-like tears that had pooled in her eyes and, with K's help, carried her to her room. This overstuffed sack of cellulite was barely capable of walking unaided. She must have weighed at least two hundred *livre*. Sweat sprang to our brows, and our flabby cargo too began to perspire, like a chunk of frozen whale meat beginning to thaw. We explained that the RED PIG had visited, and regaining a repellent arrogance, she laughed through her nose. "MADAME, S referred to you as Mariko. According to him, you used to be beautiful," explained K, to which the individual concerned responded merely, Hmm, and narrowed her eyes, which gleamed like stainless steel butcher knives buried in a desert of blubber. What those eyes were looking at, it was impossible to know. This was not a good sign. The neighbors whispered that the MADAME had lost her mind. The old man from the neighborhood watch committee would gesture at our house with his chin, point to his ear and make a spiraling motion with his finger. But no one knew whether the MADAME had truly gone crazy. Not even you, Doc, could have diagnosed her. What is certain is that, when I looked at the MADAME, cracks formed in the vessel of my consciousness, and I feared my sanity too might slip. K and I discussed it on many occasions: What has become of the OLD BAG's spirit? Has it shriveled up like a walnut in the corner of her mind, or has it spread itself thin across her vast, fleshy expanse? No, said K, I think perhaps that bulging bag of flesh itself is her spirit.

That evening, shortly after I returned from swimming in the pool at Inokashira Park, we had visitors, the woman who served as the neighborhood *shūsenya*, accompanied by a college girl who, it seemed, wished to rent the downstairs boarders' quarters. The OLD BAG stared dumbly at this peddler-cum-realtor, the Great Plain of her chest exposed, sweat trickling down her bosom. I thought to myself, barely suppressing a smile, it was apparent at a glance that the OLD BAG was deranged.

"A short while ago, you made a mistake in your locution," the OLD BAG accused sharply.

"Oh my, have I said something to offend?" asked the woman, flustered.

"Indeed: *abbartement*, *abbartement*. Have you forgotten?"

"I may have been discussing the *appartement* earlier today."

"Yes, that is correct. But yesterday, I heard you say *abbartement*. I remained silent out of politeness. But for someone like you, a graduate of a women's junior college, to make a mistake like that, it's simply unseemly. You should enunciate more carefully."

It was far from the first time I had heard her deliver such a lecture. Watching from the side of her eye as the realtor stiffened like a snake struggling to swallow an egg of shame, the OLD BAG discussed with the schoolgirl the particulars of the rent, the deposit, and so on, making no attempt to conceal a smirk. When it came to money, the OLD BAG was more precise and explicit than any Imperial University archaeological report. But as she zigged and zagged between topics—how to change babies' NAPPIES, how to tamper with the meter to get free gas—repeatedly dropping the thread of the conversation and picking it back up, I watched as the realtor and the schoolgirl repeatedly half-stood and bowed slightly to the OLD BAG as if to leave, while the OLD BAG merely looked to the side with an expression of feigned ignorance, throwing her voice like a ventriloquist, humming a bizarre ditty. Some sort of hymn, no doubt. Just as the visitors were departing, the OLD BAG remarked, loud enough to be overheard, "A young woman with a bright future. She even took pains not to step on the cracks in the tatami. That agent, on the other hand, she's old, but age hasn't made her wise."

When I climbed the stairs to my room and looked outside, I could see the agent and the schoolgirl animatedly discussing something: Surely you wouldn't think of moving in with that ghastly hag. That must have been the gist of it. In any case, the next day, the schoolgirl moved in with us, dragging along a battered old organ.

When she came to greet K and me in our shared room, I could see that she was taken aback by the sight of our half-naked bodies reclined atop the books and magazines strewn across the floor. "Don't be afraid. Come in and join us," I invited, shoving aside the scraps of paper and magazines with a foot, clearing a place for her to sit. Shall I explain about the room? K and I had resided in this room, which resembled the brain of a person with bipolar disorder, since our birth. I had spent a week pulling book after book from our voluminous library, casting each aside, until the mountain of books collapsed upon itself, and ever since, sentimentally attached to this chaos, we had been competing to adorn the room with books and rubbish and bits of paper. What sweet pleasure it was to lurk amid the dust and wastepaper with K, the soles of our feet and our elbows soiled, living like BLATTODEA, indulging in smutty talk and other illicit pleasures. It was summer, and I typically wore only a slip, K only underwear. It felt good to roll about atop the cool books.

I asked the schoolgirl her name, and she responded that it was Yukari. "But strictly speaking, not 'Yukari.' You have to pronounce it like *eucaly*. That is the wonderful and tricky thing about my name," she explained. Under her guidance, we practiced pronouncing "Yukari" dozens of times, but still couldn't get it right. Giving up hope, she declared, "The two of you are tone-deaf." But she quickly regained her cheerfulness, asking if it was true that we were a couple.

"You sound just like the OLD BAG," remarked K with a laugh.

"The madame, you mean?" asked Yukari. "Yes, she's the one who said so."

"She is our mother. You may call her the OLD BAG, as we do."

"So you're brother and sister."

"Twins. A curious pair, some say."

With this, Yukari took a sudden interest in K. In the tone of an indignant PTA member, she hurled words of reproach at him, particularly in regard to his brazen nakedness in the presence of a young lady, before retreating to her first-floor room. "You've got her worked up into a lather," I pointed out. Sooner or later, I went on, maybe today, maybe tomorrow, she would seize on some serious-minded pretext, steal in, and surrender her raw rubbery virginity to K. K expressed wholehearted agreement, and we squealed and chortled in delight.

What about the secretary position, you ask? I ended up taking it. The day after S, that is, the RED PIG, came to visit, I reported for my first day of work at the publishing company. The workload was light, and S had promised a hefty salary, so it seemed bearable, even though what I despise more than anything is work. Being a female secretary is an especially dreadful job. It wasn't my responsibility to file papers—it fell to a male secretary, a rotund man like a dragonfly's compound eye who had been at the company for many years, to complete that task. I too was assigned a grand office with a hulking steel desk and filing cabinet atop a moss-colored carpet, and a gas water heater and sideboard nestled in the corner. My main responsibilities were talking to S on the intercom, ushering authors and others to S's office, sorting mail S didn't care to open, making phone calls, and serving iced coffee or gin fizz to the executive suite when called upon. When I had free time, I spent it reading novels put out by the publisher or filing my nails. On the afternoon of the third day, S had a lunch date with a Frenchman at a *brasserie* in Tamura-chō, and I was asked along, as I can speak some French. I quickly became accustomed to this cultured lifestyle.

One day, I was listlessly staring at my face in the mirror when the RED PIG burst in, a cigarette pressed between his lips. It's about time you learned to make martinis, he said, pulling bottles of dry gin and French vermouth from the sideboard, pouring the liquor into a tumbler, and beginning to shake. Still standing before the mirror, poised hesitantly with shoulders shrugged, I took a tentative sip. I watched as the RED PIG approached, his face appearing in the mirror beside mine: this striking portrait might have been called "Beauty and Red Pig." And yet, when I smile with my lips pursed—like this, look—I resemble a ravenous, carnivorous beast. I may give the impression of a well-bred bourgeois girl, but watch, when I bend my back a bit, can't you catch a glimpse of feline nobility, something fluid and untamed? As you run your eyes over my oval-shaped face, delicate hands, and lithe figure, you can see, can't you, that I was born into a chosen family? But within the veins of nobles flows barbarian blood—so S said then.

"There's something different about you, something strange and wild."

"I'm a savage stranded in the city."

"The lost descendant of a tribe of cannibals, is that it?"

"I am indeed descended from cannibals."

"Maybe you aren't cut out to be a secretary. If you're the first thing people see when they walk in, they'll smirk when they look at me. What I mean to say is, you stand out."

The RED PIG's expression turned suddenly serious. I sensed he was on the verge of squeezing me in his arms, perhaps planting a kiss on my lips. Determined to avoid such an inevitably awkward, flubbed kiss, I turned my face away, and the RED PIG pretended nothing had happened. "What do you say, want to go for dinner together?" he whispered. "If you wish to invite me out, let's go now. My stomach is rumbling." The RED PIG's come-on had immediately aroused in me a ravenous hunger. When I stated this, the RED PIG got a bewildered look, explaining that he had an appointment with an author named G. "But it won't take more than half an hour, and your work for the day is done. Send the driver home and wait in the car."

I touched up my makeup and left. Until recently, K and I had driven the battered '53 Chevrolet we had inherited, along with the estate and some stocks, from our late father. We had driven the car to a demonstration at the Diet building and abandoned it, and some student protestors had overturned it and set it on fire. The RED PIG's car was an air-conditioned Mercedes, a vehicle with the dignified bearing of a European countess. I sent the driver home and took the car for a joyride. I love cars so much it sends shivers down my spine. Plying the surging crowds with the windows rolled up tightly, people streaming by on all sides, I loved that I could belt out gospel songs, shriek like a rape victim, and giddily give voice to my most licentious desires, which I had been saving for just such a moment: K, how I long to uncover my NAKEDNESSE to thee . . . this phrase has a special meaning which I will explain later.

By the time I remembered S, nearly an hour had passed. I circled back on the highway to the building where I had started out to find the RED PIG stamping in righteous indignation like a noble baron robbed by a highwayman. He climbed into the seat beside me and launched into a tongue lashing, sounding more like a father than a CEO. "Spare me," I spat.

I first met Q at a restaurant in Roppongi. The RED PIG and I were sitting at the table waiting on hors d'oeuvres when a boy walked in, accompanied by a girl whom I took for a college student. "There they are," said Q, waving to the RED PIG, who wore an undisguised scowl. It seemed the curtain was about to open on an ugly drama. Turning to me, he said by way of introduction, "My son." Like all young men from middling, monied backgrounds, Q fancied himself a playboy, but he was in fact a naïve, charmless lad, with a girlfriend whose naiveté and charmlessness nearly outdid his. On learning I was S's new secretary, he dropped any pretense of politeness with me.

"Aren't you going to go to college? What are you doing with your life?"

"Amusing myself," I replied. Q nodded, pretending to understand, but he persisted in asking about my reasons for not attending university.

"Listen up, you numbskull kid. L and her brother K are famous. Until last year, they were leaders of the All-Japan Student Association," said S, to which Q shrugged as if to say, Who cares? Meanwhile, the schoolgirl wilted visibly.

"There's nothing wrong with being a secretary," she piped up. "If I needed a part-time job, I'd be a secretary, too."

"The truth is that being a secretary is hard work," remarked the RED PIG with a chuckle. "Excuse me," he said, and got up to go to the toilet. It was then that Q drew in close.

"The truth is that being my father's secretary is hard work. What I mean is, he'll make quick work of you."

I responded that all CEOs, all important people, were the same, and I worked still quicker, at which point Q flashed a broad, ignorant smile, flashing his teeth, and loudly guffawed.

Several days later, a phone call came from Q. We met at an extremely dark café with COMMUNAL SEATING meant to create intimacy among strangers. Q explained that he had grown tired of the schoolgirl and wouldn't mind giving me a spin. Nearly nothing was visible in the almost total darkness, but he was sitting close enough that I was able to make out a pair of gleaming eyes and a face like those of a HORNED OWL. Seconds later, Q leaned in, and I frantically ducked. He sat for a moment in sullen silence. "So did my dad ever make a pass at you?" he asked. "Not successfully," I responded. "He has made several fumbling attempts at an *embrasse*, but each time I have had to struggle not to laugh."

"That makes me feel better."

"Not so fast. He's going to Europe in the fall. You knew that, right? He says he's taking me along."

Q clicked his tongue and at the same time snapped his fingers. Sensing he was on the verge of exploding with anger, I continued, "Don't be mad. He says if you finish your graduation thesis over the summer, you can tag along."

Next, Q invited me to a bar and began telling me about his family. I could hardly imagine a less interesting conversation topic. Boys always tell you about their families, especially their mothers, as a prelude to proposing marriage. Next, they paint a portrait of their ideal future families, the wife taking the mother's place. Then, they inevitably grab your hand. But talk of other people's families bores me senseless. When Q finished telling me about his family, he said he wanted to meet mine and declared that he would be inviting himself over.

"Out of the question," I said.

"Why?"

"K and I keep an unusual pet, a woman. She is as fat as a Yorkshire terrier, with a protruding belly. When she walks, she cradles her stomach and waddles cautiously. At times she lets her guard down, transforming into a rotund, legless creature like a DARUMA."

"What a woman, or should I say, what a beast! Is she a servant girl?"

"Oh, no. She's an invalid, with a bad heart. Other than caring for herself, she doesn't work. She occasionally makes her mind up not to move and remains in bed for days. When a visitor arrives, she lurches toward the entryway, breathing hard through her nose. Two or three times a month, she goes shopping for food. She inevitably makes a nuisance of herself, gets picked up by the police. She'll drag herself home, arms entwined with a patrolman's."

"So she just lies around?"

"As she is an amorphous puddle of flesh, it is impossible to say whether she is sitting or lying. And she's constantly praying. She has been a Christian since she was a girl."

"An admirable lady."

"By no means. When she prays, she emits inhuman grunts and groans for a minimum of two hours. There is little doubt she is out of her mind. When she talks, she lifts her right shoulder and stares at you cockeyed. Her eyes are like snakes'. Scarier, even."

"Is she violent?"

"No. But sometimes she suddenly says things that send chills down your spine. Lewd things."

"Why don't you kick her out?"

"That won't do. She's my mother."

It was late July. As these asinine dates with Q continued, though S had been behaving respectably in the office, we got in the habit of kissing good morning. One day, I returned home early from work and entered our room to find K and Yukari passionately caressing one another. Outraged, I drove her from the room, turned to K, and said the following:

"You know better than to let her in here."

"She came in on her own."

"She's fallen for you, I know it."

"She's studying English at N University."

"So what?" I spat. "If you want to hook up, do it on campus, or at a love hotel. There, you can lick and suck to your hearts' content, just don't do it in our room. I'll admit, this puppy love of yours is actually kind of cute—if you weren't such a miserable kisser, it might go somewhere."

"Ah!" K roared, tossing a half-eaten plum at me. "At least I'm not the RED PIG's personal concubine. I see you've learned from the OLD BAG how to get ahead in life."

"You saucy scamp!" I roared, biting into the plum and lobbing it back. It struck K in the eye. "Do you actually like her back? Well, do you? You can think of her while you M right here in the room, I don't care, but she can't come in."

To M means to conduct the male ritual of self-pleasure—it is in this way that we refer to it between ourselves. K, who had been rubbing the eye struck by the plum, suddenly lunged at me, and I leapt out of the way and began running, flapping my arms wildly like a chicken being chased around a coop. The buzzer-like groan of the OLD BAG was heard below. It seemed she was sounding an alarm, having detected the scuffle in our room, but we were inured to her ways, and had perfected the art of silent battle. By "battle," I am referring to TICKLE FIGHTING. Want me to show you, Doc? This is how we do it. But don't laugh—whoever laughs first loses. In any case, both K and I were ascended masters in the art of tickling, and as the tickler's hand slowly neared, like a SEA ANEMONE's desiring tentacle, the ticklee would already be rolling on the floor shrieking wildly. That day, I lost, and I rolled on the floor like a child who has eaten a PETTICOAT MOTTLEGILL. Next, as always, we played BANDIT. In this game, the loser in the tickle fight was stripped of possessions, tied up, and forced to endure any indignity the winner deemed fit. This form of play had enthralled us since childhood. I was bound tightly, writhing atop the scattered magazines, when I was struck by a pang of hunger, and devoured a grape from K's outstretched hand. Just then, K said, "I think the OLD BAG is watching." I relegated the role of checking if the OLD BAG was lurking at the door to K, who hesitated. "I don't wanna. She's obviously there." No doubt, coming eye to eye with her through the keyhole would be a blood-chilling experience for anybody, and I too would have refused. I strained to listen and was convinced I heard a sound like a giant SLUG oozing its way downstairs ... no doubt, we were being watched. K declared he would not stand for this, and we set off together for the OLD BAG's room on the first floor.

"What were you doing just now, MADAME?" K demanded. "I'm about to have dinner. Would the two of you care to join?" With this, the OLD BAG flashed a ghastly grin, her nose and the corners of her eyes crinkling. Of course, we said as one, "No, thank you." A sickening stench wafted over us, and we suppressed the urge to simultaneously cry and vomit; surely we ought to have immediately retreated. Oh yes, I should say a bit about the OLD BAG's diet. A typical meal consisted of a Kümmelbrot loaf shaped like a rugby ball and a *pot-au-feu* of birds' and animals' heads. Just then, a soup simmered in an oversized pot: upon a surface layer of golden fat bobbed a dozen-odd birds' heads, staring with hideous, hateful eyes, beaks gaping. On other occasions I glimpsed oddly shaped skulls that could have been those of pigs or dogs swirling in the steaming slurry. Later, in fact, Yukari once fainted upon seeing such a scene. The OLD BAG glanced at us pridefully as she ladled a chicken's head and vegetables into a soup bowl.

"Look and learn. A balanced diet is the key to a long life," said the OLD BAG in the tone of an elementary school teacher, flinging a bird's head into her gaping maw and chomping down. The skull crunched heartrendingly as it was pulverized; shortly, in the form of a mouthful of splintered bone fragments, it was ejected back into the bowl. "Want some?" asked the OLD BAG. "I see you'd rather die young. Well, God will come down from heaven and suck your breath out soon enough. I'm planning on sticking around." Pasting on an innocent smile, I said, "Is that so?" The OLD BAG: "Yes, your sins are plain to see, even to an illiterate idiot."

"You ought to know, MADAME," K jumped in. "You were peeping on us, weren't you? Did you like what you saw?"

Looking into K's eyes, recognizing in them a shared resolve to find a final solution without delay, I grabbed the OLD BAG and hurled her to the floor. The OLD BAG muttered unintelligibly, writhed like a capsized LOGGERHEAD, looked on stupidly as we laughed until our strength was spent. Then we tore her clothes off and carried out the sentence, lashing of the buttocks. The truth is that we did such things as often as two to three times weekly, and if the OLD BAG was at all bothered, she showed no sign. As the OLD BAG crawled like some four-legged animal, K and I took turns administering the beating, each blow drawing forth a high-pitched, flute-like shriek. Needless to say, we glimpsed the dark crevice within her ample loins, that hole through which the two of us had crawled into the world. Picture it, Doc, this vessel of our birth, this wife of a wealthy businessmen, this honorary trustee of a Catholic girls' college, thrashed and degraded at our hands. We ourselves could hardly believe what we were seeing. Her ample posterior quaked incessantly as we walloped it. The flogging drew forth shocking crimson welts, and then we grew tired, and rested. K mounted her like a horse, spurring her by slapping her buttocks with both hands like some percussion instrument, but I said, She's finished for today, give it up. Further exertion indeed proved futile, and as I looked down at this bizarre lump curled into the fetal position on the floor, I felt my hope evaporating, and I longed to crawl back into that womb where there was no light and again become my unborn self. But K, it seemed, intended to pummel this lump until it gave up its methane gas-like ghost, and persisted mercilessly, eyes flashing. Sadly, the prospects of success are slim, I informed him, but he continued trampling the OLD BAG who, seemingly on the brink of being done in, was letting out sickening groans. K ultimately admitted that victory would not be achieved today, but said he was confident a final solution would soon be reached. What did he mean by that, you ask? Let me explain, Doc.

One morning in mid-August, S paged me to announce that the trip to Europe was off, for now, though perhaps it would be possible to reschedule for next summer. I was deeply disappointed, but more so enraged, seized by the urge to leap on the RED PIG and bite him on the nose. Hope had been dangled before K and me like bait on a hook, then whisked away. "You filthy liar. Don't think I'll let you off that easy," I bellowed. The RED PIG raised his hands in the air, pleading innocence, promising to make it up to me. He said he had been browsing a foreign travel magazine when the fjords of Scandinavia and the North Sea coast of Denmark had piqued his interest. So this summer, he explained, he wanted to spend ten days on the coast of Hokkaido, some desolate stretch of shore similarly untouched by human hands—after gorging on every sort of luxury, this was the sort of genuine extravagance that could still arouse his craving. He flashed the smile of a rich egoist, and I responded with a contemptuous guffaw.

"What do you say, will you go with me?"

"Just the two of us?"

"If that's alright with you."

"A risqué proposition."

"What do you mean?"

"In savage lands, one civilized traveler may kill and consume another."

"Oh, I'd like to take a bite of you, too," said the RED PIG cheerfully, but what the oaf failed to understand was that if anyone was to be devoured, it was him.

"Well, my condition is that K goes along," I said. "And we can bring Q too, can't we?"

"I'll have to think about it." The RED PIG's disappointment was plain.

One night, I returned to our room in the dark and peered through the keyhole, as the MADAME had. I spied the image of a naked K, supine atop the scattered books, proud Pharos sparkling like a knife protruding from his loins. Never before had I had the good fortune to witness this splendid ritual. The hand conducting the ceremony gripped loosely, lovingly caressing IT—perhaps intending to gather dreams from the ether, to rub this Aladdin's lamp and summon forth a genie. This Pharos, of course, was the embodiment of K's ego, the tumescence at the core of his being. I longed to lay my hand on it, but surely K would not have permitted me. I observed as K's dreams grew full and rigid in his hand. Then, suddenly, I flung the door open. K seemed taken aback, but only after a long moment did he rise to his feet and turn upon me the languid gaze of an awakened dreamer.

"Explain to me what you were doing just now, and who you were thinking about while doing it."

"A nobody. Some wench."

"Liar."

"Yukari."

"Liar."

"Are you implying it was you? Alright, it was. It always is. Why do you have to ogle me?"

"You shabby, shameless rogue. Your eyes were like those of a possessed shaman. Don't hold back for my sake—keep at it until you finish. I'm going to change my clothes and go out."

"No need to leave. It's your room, too," said K sullenly. "But since there's no privacy in here, apparently, I get to watch."

"Take a good look," I spat, slipping my bra down over my shoulders. "But keep away. You're sweaty."

The truth is that I was afraid. Paralyzed by my own awareness of this fear, I stood frozen before the mirror. K pounced like a wolf from behind, sinking his teeth into my neck. Enraged, I turned to shove him off, and we became entangled in a combative *embrasse* resembling Greco-Roman wrestling. I attempted to toss K to the floor, but it was instead I who tumbled, a sudden pain flaring in my flank. "Are you okay?" K lifted me in his arms. I went limp over his knee, chest and neck bent backward, eyes shut. "Do you remember? When we were little, we would bathe together, and we would wash each other's hair, like this."

Then, without warning, K kissed me. It was not the sort of impish kiss one sibling might plant on another's cheek or forehead in a moment of play, but a kiss like a mouthful of cold, raw fish. Suddenly excited, I dug my nails into the hollow between K's scapulae. A long moment passed, and still K made no move to release me, so I elbowed him aside and reached for the bookshelf, pulling down an oversized Bible. There was something I needed to say to him. With a colored pencil, I drew a scarlet outline around Leviticus, Chapter 18. "Jehova's words to Moses. Read." K, still naked, sat up cross-legged and began reading aloud. I've memorized the passage. Here it is:

> None of you shall approche to any that is neere of kinne to him, to vncouer their nakednesse: I am the Lord. The nakednesse of thy father, or the nakednesse of thy mother, shalt thou not vncouer: she is thy mother, thou shalt not vncouer her nakednesse ... The nakednesse of thy sister, the daughter of thy father, or daughter of thy mother, whether shee be borne at home, or borne abroad, euen their nakednesse thou shalt not vncouer. The nakednesse of thy sonnes daughter, or of thy daughters daughter, euen their nakednesse thou shalt not vncouer: for theirs is thine owne nakednesse. The nakednesse of thy fathers wiues daughter, begotten of thy father, (she is thy sister,) thou shalt not vncouer her nakednesse ... Defile not you your selues in any of these things ... Ye shall therefore keepe my Statutes and my Iudgements, and shall not commit any of these abominations ... For whosoeuer shall commit any of these abominations, euen the soules that commit them, shall be cut off from among their people ... I am the Lord your God.

"K, do you understand? If you do, say, 'Amen.'" Together, we said it: "Amen." Then, swept away by a flood of laughter, we collapsed on the floor. Who would've guessed a moral code could be so uproarious? These drolly explicated reasons were pure poppycock, and yet, to "vncouer the NAKEDNESSE," isn't that a masterful translation?

"This is no laughing matter, K. We have committed an abomination." I tried to say it with a straight face but failed. K too was laughing so hard he seemed to be going into SPASMS. "We've got to show this to the OLD BAG," he said.

"What? The Bible?"

"The two of us uncovering our NAKEDNESSE."

I looked him over briefly. Shards of laughter shimmered in his eyes, but then they faded, and I was struck by fear. It was true, I longed to bare my NAKEDNESSE to K. I flipped again through the giant Bible, coming to this passage: "'And if any mans seede of copulation goe out from him, then hee shall wash all his flesh in water, and bee vncleane vntill the Euen.' That's biblical wisdom, K. You too ought to uphold the Lord's hygiene code."

"Don't stop there, keep reading," K shot back. "'And if a woman haue an issue, and her issue in her flesh be blood, shee shall bee put apart seuen dayes: and whosoeuer toucheth her, shall bee vncleane vntil the Euen.' Got that? You're seven times dirtier than me."

We spent the evening hurling vile verbal abuse at one another, scouring the Bible for amusing passages and reading them out loud. Ever after, K felt free to release his SEED OF COPULATION even in my presence, and I attended these ceremonies generally in the spirit of a stolid heathen, occasionally feigning astonishment or even reaching out to caress K's inflamed EFFIGY. Each time I extended a hand, however, he shrank from my touch.

A date was set for the trip, and airline tickets were booked. It was later that day that Yukari arrived on our doorstep, eyes swollen from crying. After confirming K was out, she said she and I needed to talk, and I allowed her to enter our room. Caressing feet which, tortured by ill-fitting heels and aberrant sitting positions, were misshapen and covered in CORNS, she asked if I knew about her and K. I feigned ignorance, telling her that if she wished to wash her feet, there would be no objections from me. Clearly annoyed, she confessed in a steely tone that she and K were lovers. I gave a hearty chuckle, and she glared at me resentfully, so I hurriedly excused myself, explaining that I had a terrible habit of laughing at inappropriate times. That may be, she pressed, but why do you find the harsh truth so funny?

"Whenever someone uses the word 'love,' all I can do is laugh," I explained. In fact, if I didn't at least laugh, this word would have made me retch, like a severe case of seasickness. "Anyway, like I said, we're in love," Yukari repeated. She demanded that I acknowledge the union. I told her that I doubted there would be any significance in such an acknowledgment, but I would comply with her wishes.

"Why are you telling me this?"

"Of course, we're getting married, hopefully."

"The two of you can do what you want. I'm in no position to grant permission, or to refuse. Why are you crying? Doesn't K want what you do?"

"When I spoke to your mother," Yukari began, scratching her toes, "she said *you* were married to K."

"Really, the OLD BAG said that?"

"Then she began heaping curses on the two of you. What she said was so disturbing I felt I too might go mad. She's absolutely out of her mind."

"What if what she said were true?"

"Impossible. That would be incest." Then a light flashed in her dull eyes, and she turned on me a look like that of a suspicious dormitory attendant.

"What did K say?" I asked.

"What he said was, 'In principle, I agree to getting engaged. But when it comes to getting married, I can't believe any marriage of mine is going to work. We can try, but it will be a bigger surprise if it doesn't go disastrously wrong, so I'm warning you, keep your expectations low. I'm twenty years old, a good enough age to marry, but I simply am not thrilled about the idea of you and L and I living together in this room. It would be an affront to male honor. At the same time, I can hardly drive her out.' So I said to him, Why don't you marry L?"

My patience fraying, I said the three of us could live together, I didn't care, and at this she lost her temper, exclaiming, That's impossible. "I mean, what about my PRIVACY?" She expressed concern for my PRIVACY as well. "The point is," said Yukari, at last coming around to her conclusion, "the solution is for *you* to get married as soon as possible. Then K too will understand that he must free himself psychologically from his sister."

With this, Yukari's tongue seemed to loosen, and she launched into a realistic description of her relationship with K. Like a psychologist conducting a Ravonal Interview, I listened quietly to the end in spite of the turmoil raging inside me. In part, I was jealous. Mainly, however, I was intensely fascinated by this love affair between her and K. I would have relished watching them make love, had they been willing.

Neither K nor I held out particularly high hopes for the trip, but the RED PIG seemed set on satisfying our every whim, allowing Q and Yukari, as K's fiancée, to accompany us. Our party of five arrived at the airport one mid-August day, a hot, dry wind blustering down the runway. We flew to Hokkaido in a large jet, and after having lunch in S City, boarded a chartered news company helicopter, arriving finally at a small fishing village named R on S Peninsula. We spent the night in a ryokan, the only accommodation in the village.

It was just past three in the afternoon. The sun still hung high in the sky, but it seemed to shine down at an obtuse angle, emitting a feeble yellow light more like that of a dwarf star than the sun. The dreary silence of the town beneath was unbroken even by the familiar din of bicycles. While the RED PIG was bathing, K and I stood at the window looking out over the ramshackle harbor. It was then that I asked K:

"Have you bared your NAKEDNESSE to Yukari?"

"Not yet," K responded. "Although orifices have been grazed, and protuberances have engorged."

To K, this seemed less a pleasureful indulgence than a form of cynical self-mortification. When I told him so, he nodded, saying that I was correct, but Yukari seemed to believe that such behavior was all but obligatory among ordinary lovers, seeing in it special significance.

"These petting sessions satisfy her, like a cat scratched beneath the chin, and she becomes quite passionate. There is a push and pull in such things, she says: this is the meaning of *donner et prendre*. In democracy, after all, men and women have equal rights. I give you fellatio, and you reciprocate with cunnilingus."

Laughing, I asked K if she had actually said these things. "Yes," he responded, absolutely straight-faced. "She has memorized them, and repeats them at least half a *douzaine* times a day. In truth, however, I would rather M than uncover my NAKEDNESSE to the likes of her."

"How charming, K. Do remain an ardent onanist," I said, inwardly fantasizing of shattering the foolish illusions of this schoolgirl who fancied herself K's lover. "And K, do you not think that this trip presents an excellent opportunity to rape a halfwit swine?"

"Most definitely."

Reclining in a rattan chair, we indulged in a brief nap. When I opened my eyes, a yellow late-afternoon light filled the room. Seized by the sudden urge to bathe in the cold northern sea, I woke K, and we ventured into town. We walked along the coastline toward the western horizon, beneath which the sun had just begun to sink. A stone stairway wound leisurely past some rundown country houses surrounded by low stone walls and down to the harbor. The air was heavy with the stench of fish, overlaid with a whiff of seaweed. I strolled through the town swathed in Italian colors the likes of which were surely a rare sight in such a place, wearing sunglasses beneath a broad-brimmed straw hat. We were soon being trailed by some dozen fishermen's children. When we stopped and looked back, they stopped as well. K picked up a stone and mimed throwing it. Such a trick may serve to ward off a cowardly dog, but the children merely dispersed to either side of the path. No one said a word.

Looking out over the harbor was like peering into the mouth of a person with no teeth. We saw several fishing boats and skiffs. This vista of the village, crude houses swarming from the gap between the squat, sepia-toned hills around the horseshoe-shaped harbor and the shore, had likely remained unchanged for half a century.

The dense, brackish daily life in which the people here were immersed had a quality entirely unlike our own, and I suspected the water that gently lapped the shore pilings might prove poisonous to me. It readily parted, with dark ripples, when I stepped in. The water was not as cold as I had imagined, but for some reason I cannot explain, it chilled me deeply. Submerged to our necks, we leisurely swam. K's face was so pale . . . I was suddenly struck by the terrifying sense that we were drifting in murky amniotic fluid. Yes, perhaps a submerged memory of K and me embracing in the OLD BAG's womb had resurfaced here, twenty years later, from the chill water of this uncanny harbor. K drew near, entwining his arms in mine. A slick tongue and teeth peered from his mouth, which parted as if to shout, but no sound emerged. When I turned my head, the children on the shore raised their hands as one and let out an indecipherable cry. Was it a cry of ecstasy, or some sinister curse? Unnerved, I nudged K, and we swam swiftly back to shore, sending up spray.

Q asked, How was your swim? "Horrible," I said. "Like bathing in toxic waste." You have to be crazy to swim in that harbor, he said, suggesting the two of us go take a bath. I declined, and it was decided that the girls would bathe together, so Yukari and I went off to the wood-paneled washroom.

Once we had removed our clothes, it struck me that Yukari was both overweight and strangely withered.

Whereas the OLD BAG had a fertile heft that exceeded the ordinary proportions of the human form, Yukari, though quite flabby, gave a flimsy, insubstantial impression. Perhaps, while clothed, tight underwear wrenched her body into an unnatural shape. Having never been in the bath with anyone except K, I had failed to acquire a knack for concealing my privates. Yukari eyed me as she scrupulously cleansed herself, making delicate, small movements. She said, I'm jealous of you because you're K's sister, and I'm jealous of your long legs. Don't monopolize K—let me have him. I don't understand your logic, but you can do whatever you want with K, I said.

"Of course I can. After all, we're engaged. And you and Q will be engaged soon too, won't you? It will all work out," said Yukari. Upon completing a thorough cleansing, she went to see K, and I, grudgingly, went to see Q. We embraced for approximately ten minutes, rolling on the floor like logs, exchanging kisses of all descriptions, but to me this exercise proved unsatisfying and ultimately annoying. Just then, the RED PIG flung open the sliding screen that separated our room from his, saying, Come have a beer with me. Between swigs, we shelled and ate a large crab. Intoxicated, the RED PIG spouted lewd comments concerning Q and me.

The next morning, I opened the window to find that the town and the harbor, bathed in golden sunlight, had undergone an astonishing rebirth. It had become an entirely different town: the ocean was a clear blue, and the sun blazed cheerily. We had planned to depart from R Village that morning, but unable to arrange a boat, we were forced to extend our stay by an additional day. In the early afternoon, leaving behind S, who had begun a game of go with the innkeeper, the four of us set out barefoot for the harbor. As before, we were trailed by fishermen's children. Q grabbed hold of one of them and said, You guys wanna go for a swim with us, or what? The boy said nothing, expressionless eyes sparkling beneath heavy lids. "They don't even understand standard Japanese. My god, we're really in the sticks," Q marveled. Yukari bent down and babbled to them in incomprehensible baby talk. I suddenly scooped a boy up in my arms. After watching me for a brief moment, he began to wail, lips twisted, but without any tears, as if he had seen a witch. We got into the ocean and swam. Suddenly, a big red dog charged through the crowd of children, leapt into the water, and began swimming toward us. As one, the children began clapping and laughing, mouths all parted in the same O shape.

Upon finishing our swim, we followed the coast to a shop in a little reed hut where we all drank *ramune*, then proceeded further along a narrow cobbled path to its terminus at a grimy bay. Dilapidated shops crowded the shoreline. In the fishmonger's storefront, mysterious fish were marooned in puddles of melted ice. When I picked one up, a large man like a red-horned demon with no eyebrows lumbered out, delivering an eager sales pitch in an almost incomprehensible patois. Don't even think about it, put that back, Q admonished. I asked how much it cost, got the money out, and paid. This light brown fish with mahogany FRECKLES like the tanned chest of Burt Lancaster squirmed as my grip around it tightened. "For you, K," I said, tossing it at him. "No thanks," he cried, flinging it back. We lobbed the fish back and forth, shrieking and laughing. Soon it was mangled and oozing gore. As we lifted our bloody hands and laughed, Q and Yukari looked on, mouths gaping.

Early the next morning, we departed from R Harbor aboard a semi-diesel fishing vessel. The boat chugged slowly along the coastline toward the tip of the peninsula. The churning sea and the steep cliffs aroused in me a morbid agitation. This bleak landscape was like none I had ever seen. The RED PIG came out to where I sat near the prow and informed me that Q and Yukari were suffering from seasickness.

"You ought to take one of these tablets, too."

"It's fine. I'm not seasick. Oh my, the ocean and the sky are both swaying . . . what's that out there? A GULL?"

"No, a MURRE. Want to shoot at it with my Winchester?"

I accepted the rifle from the RED PIG, aimed, and pulled the trigger. The shot rang out, the sky and the clouds quaked, and the recoil stole my breath.

"Did I hit it?"

"Hahaha. Try keeping your eyes open next time."

The RED PIG grabbed the gun in a practiced motion and fired several shots into the water where the MURRE had dived in. It emerged shortly, belly up.

"We need to talk about you and Q," said the RED PIG, offering a cigarette. I accepted, and he lit it. His expression turned suddenly serious. "Q told me he is in love with you. How do you feel?"

The RED PIG had employed European translationese to speak straightforwardly of being IN LOVE, demonstrating himself to be a cultured gentleman. I responded, I don't know what love is, but if I were in love, what would you think?

"You seem upset about it. Well then, let's say I'm not in love."

"What's that supposed to mean?" the RED PIG grumbled. "The point is, you're a shrewd, sensible woman, but Q is still a kid. He may be older, but he doesn't understand people the way you do. To Q, this is a very serious matter. We were discussing it last night, and he even mentioned marriage. He is certainly in a terrible hurry. By the sound of it, I'm assuming the two of you have slept together—would I be right?"

"Of course," I lied cheerfully.

"I see. If my son knocked you up, please, allow me to cover the expenses—that should be a hundred thousand yen at least up front. And if you're interested in an ongoing arrangement with me, that'll be an extra hundred thousand a month." The RED PIG flashed a semblance of a smile, a deep furrow forming in his brow, the corners of his lips curling, revealing sparkling golden crowns. This villain with the face of a bloated Al Capone made a worthy rival, I reflected, fighting spirit aroused. His point was that he would not allow Q and me to marry. The reason, he remarked, was that at present, the class difference between the S family and mine was too great.

"I want my son to marry well, like any parent. But the idiot kid won't listen. So I'd appreciate it if you'd quash this budding love of his. I'll see that you want for nothing." Again, the RED PIG smiled, the corners of his eyes quivering spasmodically. I pasted on a cutesy look, crinkling the tip of my nose, suppressing the murderous hostility already beginning to crystallize inside me. Then, I said this: "I choose you. I'd love to stick a slickline into you and pump out all the money I can. I'll do anything if you let me suck you dry."

In places, dunes spilled over the jutting bluffs. On one such narrow strip of sand stood two or three fishermen's cabins. According to the local fishermen, these served in summer as inns but were cut off from all land and sea transport in winter. Many years ago, some shipwrecked sailors had washed up on the shore and wintered there, and when the snow melted, the captain alone had escaped by scaling the mountain. When the rescuers arrived, they found only scattered bones marked with the impressions of teeth. On hearing this, Yukari turned pale and shrieked, KYAAA!

The boat proceeded up an inlet through a gap in the cliffs. We docked at the foot of a dune where a large cabin stood. With help from the fishermen, we unloaded our luggage and carried it inside. In addition to rations, our cargo consisted of newly purchased camping supplies, propane cylinders, a culinary workbench, and folding beds. Two playful greyhounds nipped at our heels as we worked. The RED PIG had borrowed the dogs from an acquaintance of his, a hunter in R Village.

On the desolate shoreline, abandoned except for us, we assembled a luxury encampment. At noon, a fisherman who lived in a nearby cabin arrived in a small boat with a fresh catch of fish. We would occasionally request fresh SEA URCHIN from the fisherman, smash it on a rock and slurp it straight from the shell. This quickly became my favorite food. I would also gather fresh kombu which washed up on the rocks. We obtained a LEISTER and began harvesting exotic shellfish, crab, and SEA URCHIN from the reefs. When the rays of the sun became too intense, we would surf and occasionally dive.

The RED PIG and the hunting dogs spent the days lying beneath a beach parasol. When the RED PIG's clothes were off, it became apparent that he was startlingly hairy: with a bulging belly and eddies of fur swirling about his navel, he looked strikingly like a stuffed bear. Noticing he nearly never entered the water, Yukari and I would grab his hands and pull, but with a puckered expression befitting a timid forty-seven-year-old man, he would refuse to advance past the shallows. The cause of this overcaution seemed to be a weak heart and high blood pressure. Thus, I often beckoned the RED PIG into the water, hoping he might drop dead, but he was too prudent to be done in in this way. K, ever the malicious bully, would seize Yukari, a middling swimmer, and force her beneath the waves, drawing forth immodest shrieks. Of course, Yukari too took pleasure in this. Q was obsessed with hunting with the LEISTER and would invite me to join him beyond the cape, claiming the prey there was more abundant. Well understanding the true nature of his quarry, I remained deliberately out of reach.

I had imagined that Q and I would eventually get around to doing what men and women did, but each time he sought me out, panting like a dog in the sweltering sun, I only barely managed to hold back laughter. On one occasion, Q accused, You don't love me, do you? I responded, When you frame the question that way, I am unable to say I do. "Of course, it is not necessary to be in love in order to make love," I asserted. At this, Q's irritation flared, like a smoldering briquette jabbed with a poker. "Then let's do it, right now," he demanded. Laughing, I said, "That isn't the way it works. You have to wait until I'm in the mood." However, intoxicated perhaps by the sun and surf, I was feeling unusually generous. One evening, for instance, Q and I left the hut and ran to the glistening cobalt sea, and I stripped off every stitch of clothing. Q did likewise. Our bodies, slick with sea spray, suddenly collided, and we tumbled together to the sand. We very nearly did make love. The problem was that when Q touched me, I suddenly became extremely ticklish. Making love was out of the question. "These giggling fits of mine are like the HICCUPS. Nothing to do but wait." Q was indignant, and simultaneously his desire for me seemed to intensify.

On the evening of our third day at the cabin, the RED PIG's driver arrived aboard the semi-diesel boat. It seemed the meeting had been planned: the following morning, the two set out to hunt in a virgin forest some twenty kilometers away, carrying their sleeping bags and rations on their backs, trailed by the dogs. "Keep this quiet, alright? We're going poaching," said the RED PIG.

"Bring back a big brown bear," urged Yukari, so I said, "More likely, the bear will lumber back to camp in a day or two with the rifle over its shoulder." Yukari was overjoyed to learn we would have several days alone with our respective lovers. I knew that with poisonous insects like K and me about, these *dolce vita* illusions would soon be stripped from her. In fact, the RED PIG's absence provided an excellent opportunity for two scorpions to run amok.

Just after noon, K and I walked along the shore to the base of a waterfall approximately two kilometers from camp, where the river spilled over a bluff into the sea. We were overjoyed to finally have a moment alone—so I say as if we were lovers, which in a way, although more similar to one another than other lovers, we were. For the first time in a long while, we stripped naked and had a TICKLE FIGHT. Oddly, however, I felt no urge to laugh. We lay on the sand, bellies exposed to the sun, listening wordlessly to the waves, when a sudden anxiety gripped me. Summer was ending, our birthday was nearing, and in spite of another year passing we continued to drift through life without direction. What we would do the next day, or even the next instant, I had no idea. We lay perpendicular to one another, heads pressed together, and I lifted my head like a cobra, my lips finding K's in an unforced kiss. I was filled with despair, and K watched me with kind eyes. Just then, K's sparkling Pharos emerged into the sun like the shoot of a plant in spring. "Excited, I see." I could not resist the urge to caress this protuberance. Before my eyes, it grew bigger than a space rocket, filling my entire world, becoming my entire world. As K surrendered this part of himself to me, I was absorbed by fantasies of transforming K's body into a plant. Ravaged by my tongue and teeth, this shoot pumped hot sap into my mouth. Following this, it softened . . . K took the lead in the ritual that followed, using his tender tongue and lips to transform me into pure carnality. As K's nimble head flitted from my breasts to my belly, from my legs to the hollow at my center, casting a spell, I became something shapeless yet weighty, and when his mouth reached the flower that blossomed in my core, the demons in my body released a poisonous gas of pleasure which gushed from my mouth like colorless flame. Then, I sank, coming to rest in a peace where there was no time.

As the long afternoon dwindled, the sun drooping low, K and I transformed back into our usual selves, exchanging hateful barbs, playing detestable pranks. We hastened to the cabin, plotting all the while, determining what was to become of Q and Yukari and the RED PIG. Filled with vitality, K declared that he would uncover Yukari's NAKEDNESSE that very evening, and I responded with enthusiastic agreement.

It was the sort of night that stirs sinister urges. Around twilight, a dense fog had risen from the sea, shot through with ribbons of vapor like the frozen atmosphere of Jupiter. I lit the kindling on the dirt floor of the cabin. "Looks like another cold night," commented Yukari. Seemingly seized by a pang of concern over his graduation thesis, Q sat by a lamp, poring over a book. Putting on a cardigan, I practically forced him to go for a walk. The misted air was dark and heavy, again suggesting Jupiter with its eddies of toxic gas. Q listened with apparent lack of interest as I spoke of Jupiter. I'd rather visit Saturn, he remarked. "At least it has pretty rings." I informed him that Saturn was every bit as depressing a planet as Jupiter. Just then, the mournful cry of a BLACK-TAILED GULL percolated through the mist. Q lifted the rifle he had been carrying and shot into the dark. He said, About time to be heading back, don't you think?

"No. The lovebirds are busy." Q screwed up his face, apparently not understanding, when something like a scream sounded, and he again shouldered his rifle. This time, it was clearly not the cry of a BLACK-TAILED GULL. Q took off running toward the cabin, and I followed breathlessly. Keep out, K is raping Yukari, I shouted. It was pitch dark inside the cabin. Repeated screams that seemed to be Yukari's assailed my ears. These ear-rending shrieks were seemingly not of protest but of fear. I'm telling you, Doc, you wouldn't believe how a schoolgirl can scream. "What the hell is going on?" demanded Q in a high-pitched voice. "It's alright. Leave them be," I said, grabbing him by the arm. The screams abruptly broke off, giving way to forlorn, protracted sighs and cries of ecstasy. "Look, she's fine," I said, shining my flashlight into the dark. There lay Yukari, limbs bent at bizarre angles.

"Now it's your turn," I said, shoving Q into the cabin. Just then, K emerged in the doorway: "All yours." I draped the cardigan over K's shoulders, as if welcoming back a war hero, and the two of us stepped outside.

"I thought those screams of hers would rip a hole in the fabric of the universe."

"No, she's the one who got a hole ripped in her. She said she was against premarital sex. What a laugh. I put a stop to her sermon with my fist, and she started into screaming, as you heard. In the morning, I will uncover her NAKEDNESSE once more, then toss her into the sea."

"An excellent idea," I agreed. "I'd be honored to help."

Yukari emerged the following morning wearing not a look of shock or humiliation, but a strangely sly smile. Thinking it over, it occurred to me that perhaps this was only natural for a female student in whose NAKEDNESSE two men had partaken. Following a strained, silent breakfast, Q confessed to me the acts he had committed the previous evening, apparently in an attempt to obtain a pardon from me. There's no need to apologize, I told him.

"By no means do I expect you to make love only to me. In fact, I am not planning on making love to you at all. It is only natural for you to seek from other women that which I am unwilling to give." But Q persisted in trying to justify himself, claiming to love me only.

"Then stop being such a goody-goody." I then asked what he thought about Yukari, now that he had had a taste of her. "She's nothing compared to you, but I suppose that kind of girl is alright."

"Then use her for a while. You and K can take turns."

Thus, for the span of two days, our cabin transformed into a den of iniquity. While the others were occupied indoors, I amused myself by the seaside. Each time, I returned to find Yukari in the *embrasse* of either Q or K. She complained ceaselessly to me, saying, "Now, if I get pregnant, no one will know who the father is." I sensed that, now that she was in a kind of relationship with two men, she had developed a twisted sense of superiority over me. She even declared that as a marriage partner, she preferred Q who, though muddleheaded, at least came from money.

On the eve of the hunting party's return, a typhoon-like wind lashed the sea, stirring tall waves. I looked into K's eyes and confirmed a silent accord: it was time to take Yukari for a swim. This tumultuous sea would make a perfect tomb. Tossing her a life preserver, we rode the high waves to the open ocean. I'll be fine with this life preserver, said Yukari, but are the two of you sure it's a good time to be swimming out to sea? No problem at all, K shouted with a smile. We'll take the life preserver on the way back. She seemed about to say something, but before she could, we pounced, K grabbing her legs, I her neck. Unable to restrain our laughter, we swallowed a large quantity of salt water as we worked. Yukari quickly went limp and was devoured by the waves. I imagined her body progressively putrefying as the tide swept it to the Sea of Okhotsk, perhaps even the Bering Sea. We arrived ashore exhausted and napped. K lay beside me on his belly. When around two hours had passed, I roused him, and the two of us began shrieking in mock horror. Q rushed from the cabin, rifle at the ready, and together we sprinted to the friendly fisherman's cabin, finding a number of fishermen gathered there. When we explained that our friend had been spirited away by the waves, they rose from where they sat, cursing loudly. They set out in a boat, but of course, given the weather, it was impossible to carry out a proper search.

"I feel partly responsible for Yukari's death," said Q that evening. "If it was suicide, I suppose the cause was that I forced things to happen with her. And if you watched her die without acting, I imagine you did so because I made you jealous. Either way, much of the blame is mine."

I had to laugh at Q's absurd seriousness. It was sad that he had lost a friend, but it had been purely an accident, it was unthinkable that Yukari could have met her end in any other way, and the idea that Q bore any responsibility was a farce, I said, in response to which Q, relieved, grabbed my hand and held tightly. In a voice heavy with grief, he stated that even though it might not be the best time, he wanted to talk seriously about marrying me.

"Sure, I'll marry you," I declared with exaggerated earnestness. "But know that your father doesn't approve. He says our family backgrounds are too different."

"Typical old man talk. Don't worry, I'll convince him."

"Not so fast, Q," said K. "S is opposed to you marrying L for a more, let's say, worldly reason. You understand, don't you? You ought to have understood a long time ago, but in case you really don't, L is your father's secretary-cum-mistress."

"What the hell is that supposed to mean?" said Q, face black with dimwitted shame. I grinned in return. Q's eye neared the tip of my nose.

"Is that true?"

"What do you think?"

"That damned animal," Q cursed, pale lips quivering with agitation. "That filthy fucking pig. I'll put another hole in that fat belly of his, this one with a bullet."

"Don't make threats you don't intend to follow through on," I said with every intention of further agitating Q. "Your talk doesn't bother him a bit. You're a baby who'd be lost without his daddy. If you weren't the son of a CEO, you'd be nothing. Even if I did like you better than the RED PIG, it wouldn't mean a thing."

"You're after my dad's money. Now I see."

"Give up on me, then."

“GODDAMN IT TO HELL,” Q spat, shoulders quaking. “I won’t let you be my father’s mistress, mark my words.” With this, he picked up the Winchester.

“Q, if you bring guns into this, you’re going to be sorry. You know your father never misses a clay pigeon at the shooting range.” Smiling innocently at Q, K shot me a glance that said, This is going to get interesting.

Having nothing else to say, we decided to sleep. Q sat for a while in silence, finger inching along the rifle’s trigger, then suddenly leapt to his feet, rushed outside and shot some dozen bullets into the dark. “I’d love to see one of those bullets blow a hole in the RED PIG’s belly,” I said to K. And I slept.

The next morning, wearing a deeply gloomy look, Q set out for the seashore with the LEISTER. After seeing him off, I pondered whether we should flee the encampment. When I shared this thought with K, he nodded and said, “Not now, but soon.” The hue of the late August sea foretold the end of summer. Between the two of us and the RED PIG and his son, there would soon be a final settling of accounts.

Late in the afternoon, heralded by the barking of dogs, the RED PIG and the driver returned. Face caked with dust and sweat, the RED PIG looked every bit the veteran hunter. He had returned with some unidentifiable birds, a hare, and a fox. This fox, the RED PIG began, when I interrupted: “We’ve got a problem. Q is angry about the marriage. He says he’s going to kill you.”

"That little shit," growled the RED PIG. Just then, Q emerged from the shadow of a beach parasol, and I scampered up a sand dune to join K, leaving behind the RED PIG, who was cleaning a hunting gun. K and I settled in to enjoy the show, reclining among the hard, dry summer grasses. K grabbed me by the hand. Eager to see tragedy unfold, his palms were slick with sweat. Q drew near the RED PIG, dragging his shadow across the sand. His right hand held the long LEISTER. They seemed to be saying something, but all we could hear from our perch was the monotonous surf.

"Is he really going to follow through?" K wondered aloud.

"Bet on it," I said, but in truth, I was not so certain. My eyes darted to the cabin—was that the barking of a dog I'd heard? The emergence of the driver and the greyhounds would put a swift end to the unfolding drama. K bit his fingernails, corundum-like eyes wide. Q continued approaching the RED PIG. The RED PIG leaned against the fence, hunting gun in hand. In the next instant, I feared, they might declare a draw, exchanging a manly pat on the back. It often happens that at the decisive moment, a tragedy turns to a farce, breaths held in suspense loosed in a torrent of mirth. "Do it," I whispered, like a magic spell. "It's no use," said K. But then Q's arm, as if guided by a marionette string, lifted the LEISTER and stabbed it into the RED PIG's chest. In the next instant, the shotgun's muzzle jolted up, and following what seemed an impossibly long silence, a gun blast sounded. The RED PIG crumpled silently to the ground, chest stained red. Q, now missing a large part of his face, collapsed much further away, a flower of blood slowly blooming over the sand where his half of a head came to rest. I watched the two dogs run toward them, followed by the driver, arms waving wildly.

A police officer from the station in R Village arrived the following morning. At the scene, which remained undisturbed, the driver explained the incident, and then the officer, a man with sharp cheekbones, asked me if I had any idea what had caused this. I do have some idea, I said. Q and I had been engaged, but S was opposed. This, I explained, had likely led to an argument which had happened to take place when both men had deadly weapons in hand. Case closed, I said, to which the officer responded that he would be the one to investigate the matter. We were transported, along with the bodies, to R Village.

The following afternoon, the RED PIG's wife arrived in the village. A handkerchief pressed to her thin, upward-slanting eyes, this slender woman hovered over Q and the RED PIG, who lay embalmed in coffins. She spilled the most tears for Q. We tried to comfort her, but she only wailed louder, blubbering between convulsive sobs that now her young daughter was all she had to live for.

The arrival of this haggard woman put an end to our diversions. K and I were quite satisfied with the results of our excursion, and banishing any remaining memories of the three victims, which were fading quickly anyway, we left for home.

It is nearly impossible to describe the scene that awaited us there. The MADAME lay on the ground, rolling in her own excrement. When asked what had become of the attendant we had hired, the MADAME responded that she had fired her. "A shameful waste of funds. Anyway, I would rather be like this than become a burden on someone." K responded by heaping ridicule upon her, informing her that this excrementitious solitude of hers was nothing noble. In fact, she retorted, this solitude of mine is absolute. Reflecting that there might be some truth in this, I urged K to get a hose, and after wetting down this mass of feculent aloneness, we scrubbed it with bathroom cleaning products and dragged it to the garden to dry in the sun.

"What do we do now?" asked K.

"I'm thinking hanging," I said. K's response, eyes sparkling: "Delightful." For a moment, we looked each other over, and I was able to confirm clearly that the desire that sparkled in K's eyes was the same as mine: we both yearned to kill for pleasure. It occurred to me that it would be most appropriate for the OLD BAG to meet her end swinging in the air, neck snapped by her own weight. For her part, she did not seem to object.

"Rope!" I cried. K disappeared into the shed, returning with a length of hemp rope. While wrapping this around the OLD BAG's neck, I recalled the custom of matricide practiced by certain tribes. When the children have reached maturity, and their mother is no longer fertile, they pour molten lead into her womb, killing her. The completion of this highly significant rite marks the children's transition to adulthood. We all yearn for vengeance against the being that excreted us into this world, do we not, Doc? You ask if our intent was to kill? Don't doubt we burned with murderous rage from the moment we were born. In fact, it was this alone that sustained us.

K and I dragged this bag of flesh that had birthed us to the HOUSE OF WORSHIP. We tickled her ceaselessly, knowing this from long experience to be the best, most efficient method to quash any futile urge to resist on her part. This caused the OLD BAG to continuously emit lewd howls like those of a crazed hyena. Tying the rope to a ceiling beam, we slid a chair under the OLD BAG, a task like forcing a flabby elephant to sit upright.

"Any last words, MADAME?" I asked. The OLD BAG drooled, staring into space, seemingly paralyzed by fear. K said with a smile, "MADAME, you are to be hung. You may object, but it is too late now. Good riddance." Then K kicked the chair, which failed to move.

"Hoist the OLD BAG higher."

With this, I pulled the chair from beneath her. It was the classic image of a hanging, the OLD BAG twirling at the end of the rope, slowly gyrating in space, but then without warning the knot slipped, and the OLD BAG crashed loudly to the ground. Our hearts sank.

"Fret not. We'll get her this time," K muttered as he retied the rope. This time all did go well.

The hung woman dangled in the air, limbs flailing spasmodically, tongue lolling out, dancing comically like some possessed marionette. We joined hands as the OLD BAG continued to dance, eyes bulging. We stared up and laughed until our necks hurt, then, still laughing, climbed the stairs to our room, where we collapsed onto the floor. Between continuing bursts of laughter, we made complete, perfect love.

Michael Day is a traveler, translator, and writer who splits his time between Los Angeles and Latin America. His translations include *Justice with a Smile* by Osamu Dazai and *Diablo's Boys* by Yang Hao (co-translation with Nicky Harman). He is the recipient of the Jules Chametzky and the Bai Meigui translation prizes.